Resonance

Resonance

Antonia Casey

Copyright © 2007 by Antonia Casey.

ISBN:	Softcover	978-1-4257-5324-5

All rights reserved. No part of this book may be reproduced or transmitted in any form or by any means, electronic or mechanical, including photocopying, recording, or by any information storage and retrieval system, without permission in writing from the copyright owner.

This is a work of fiction. Names, characters, places and incidents either are the product of the author's imagination or are used fictitiously, and any resemblance to any actual persons, living or dead, events, or locales is entirely coincidental.

This book was printed in the United States of America.

To order additional copies of this book, contact:
Xlibris Corporation
1-888-795-4274
www.Xlibris.com
Orders@Xlibris.com

For P., with heartfelt gratitude for inspiring me
to take on this project,
for guiding me along the way,
and for pushing me to see it through to the end.

" . . . time and space mean nothing . . ."

P1

I can see now that getting drunk kept me functioning as well as I did for as long as I did. Alcohol silenced the doubts and the derision rattling around inside my head, so I could get up and go to work in the morning ready to face another day. That wasn't always an easy thing for me to pull off, so I guess I was lucky I had booze to keep me going. Liquor worked like a local anesthetic for me; whenever my symptoms flared up, I would apply it liberally to the affected area and the pain would subside.

Usually, this would happen at night. During the day, I could disappear into my work. My job provided me with the perfect escape route from my own head. That was lucky, too. Because I was an actor, I could spend most of the day in someone else's skin. I was in the business of bringing certain parts of myself to a character and leaving the rest behind. It was the nights that gave me the most trouble.

The darker side of things always held a certain fascination for me. I probably wrote a lot more angst-ridden poetry than the average teenager. Even as a little kid, I remember taking my responsibilities as the oldest child very seriously. It wasn't that I didn't know how to have fun, but I always held back just the slightest bit from getting completely carried away. I wished I could have been blessed with a sunnier nature, and as an adult I continued to envy that in other people. When I got old enough for romance, I searched for a woman who could help me find that lightness within myself.

Of course, all that intensity was very useful to me in my work. I had a lot of material to call upon when I started studying the Method approach, and I continued to draw from that well throughout my career. It seems like a contradiction but, although I would have liked to be more easy-going and carefree in my real life, I did not particularly enjoy portraying that kind of character. I much preferred being the heavy and I found it easier to play those kinds of roles, probably because I had more in common with those characters temperamentally. I also believed those performances would be taken more seriously by people in the business who could help advance my career. I had definite ideas about what I wanted to do professionally, and my vision of the future did not include bouncing from one TV sitcom to another with time off for an occasional made-for-TV movie.

Earnestness was pretty typical of those times, so while I admit that I had a tendency to take myself a little too seriously, I certainly was not alone in this. The war in Vietnam was going on, and people my age truly wanted to make the world a better place. There were all kinds of countercultural ways of looking at things and approaches to try out. It was not in my nature to do anything half way, and the feverishness of that socially conscious climate made my commitment to my particular cause, protecting the environment, even stronger. It also made me tougher on myself, because we all expected so much of ourselves back then. There was not a lot of room for compromise or shades of gray; things were very clearly right or wrong, good or bad, and so were people. It was easy to fall short of such an exacting yardstick.

I drank because I didn't have the guts to face all the ways that I didn't measure up. But I wasn't proud of being such a coward, so all the time that I was numbing myself with booze, I was feeling bad about having to numb myself with it. The worse I felt about myself, the more I drank; the more I drank, the worse I felt. Then I would go to work and "act" like a normal person. At night, I had to face that weak failure in the mirror with the glass in his hand, whom no amount of recycling could redeem. Smoking pot never seemed like a character flaw to me the way drinking did because it wasn't something I did alone, in the dark, until I couldn't feel anything. Plus, pot was considered cool by my generation, while liquor was looked down upon as one of the older generation's hang-ups. So I saw myself as a sell-out as well as a failure. But I kept right on drinking anyway.

D1

Year after year, the sounds of the neighborhood floated up the street to her house at the top of the hill. In the summer, the crack of a baseball bat against a ball cut through the high-pitched clamor of children's voices. In the winter, the whiz of snowballs and the whoosh of sled blades whispered past their excited screams. In fall, leaves crunched under new Buster Brown school shoes and in spring, go-cart wheels rumbled down the pavement. Kids stood outside front doors singing out their friends' names, inviting them out to play; mothers stood on front porches, calling them back in for dinner. Four Seasons songs buzzed through the AM-band static of transistor radios, until Beatles albums hissed and crackled around turntables. Motown wafted out the windows of station wagons, until Jimi Hendrix burst into flames in stereo.

Denise evolved over time as well. At first, A-line mini-dresses and tiger-print bellbottoms, day-glo face paint and love beads were her main concerns. As the political assassinations, protest marches, and drug overdoses piled up, her priorities began to shift. And when her 18-year-old neighbor stepped on a land mine in Vietnam, everything came into focus for her. The image of his waxy, reassembled face under the glass partition that covered his casket would not leave her. Beatle posters came down off her bedroom walls, and peace signs and political slogans went up. She started hanging out on the New Haven Green, attending anti-war demonstrations and ecology teach-ins. Before long, non-violent protest began to seem futile, and she found herself secretly applauding the radical activities of the Weather Underground.

At the same time that she was struggling to find a way through the social and political turmoil swirling around her, Denise was navigating the mundane waters of teenage romance. Shortly before he left for college, the object of her first serious crush told her, "You know, I just want a girl who's always smiling—even when she's not." Denise was not interested in non-stop cheerleading on the sidelines of someone else's life. She cared too passionately about too many of the important issues of the day to keep a silly grin on her face all the time just to make someone else feel comfortable. But at seventeen, she lacked the confidence to defend herself. She took his words at face value and felt duly rejected.

Her teenaged self-image was like the nesting Tupperware bowls her mother sold part-time to other housewives at suburban house parties. The small pastel green bowl contained her ability to excel in school without really trying, and the medium-sized pink bowl held the political radicalism and rebel heart that were her claims to high school fame. But the large yellow bowl was full of the ways that she was not good enough, and although airtight seals kept everything safely compartmentalized, the yellow bowl easily swallowed the other two whole. Once the excess air was released, the three pieces became one indivisible set.

She started dating a long-haired burger-flipper from the local McDonald's named Remy, who never said a word about whether or not she ought to smile more often. He just wanted to get into her pants, and he especially liked the idea of getting there before anyone else. Denise went along with him because she was sick and tired of being a virgin. All the stopping and starting and resisting and yielding had become a real drag. Once it was over, she could hardly wait for him to leave so that she could call her best friend, Doreen, and tell her all about it.

On the way back to her house one night a few months later, Remy was pulled over for driving with a broken tail light. In a flash, he grabbed the pot he had stashed under his seat and crammed it into her suede-fringed handbag. When they arrived at her door, having escaped with just a warning, Denise handed the aromatic baggie back to him and told him not to call her anymore. She had a quick fling with her cousin Charlie and a few one-night-stands with boys whose names she quickly forgot. Then both she and Doreen made it with the stock boy at the Marshall's department store where they all had summer jobs. Before long, this sort of activity became a drag as well. Denise refocused her attention again, and went back to looking for ways to help bring an end to the war, clean up the environment, and get ready for the coming revolution.

P2

I grew up in Patterson, a small town in northeastern Pennsylvania surrounded by acres of pristine woodland and close to ancient, worn-down eastern mountains that seemed higher and craggier to us kids than any other mountains could possibly be. Small town life at that time was a lot like the small town life I read about in children's books by Robert McCloskey. Everybody knew everybody else, and everyone had a job that contributed directly to the smooth functioning of the community. There was so little crime that the town was able to get by with just one constable, one judge, and two lawyers who spent a lot more of their time handling civil matters than defending felons. My family had provided several generations of doctors, all of whom treated patients from cradle to grave and made house calls.

My parents met when my father was an intern at the hospital in Scranton where my mother worked as a nurse. They were married just before the United States entered World War II, and my mother was pregnant with me when my father shipped out to serve as a Navy medical officer in the Pacific. He served two fifteen-month tours of duty, with just enough leave time in between to father a second child, my brother Greg. After the war my little sister, Penny, was born.

We had a lot of good times growing up in Patterson, mostly outdoors. Television was not yet the constant presence in people's homes that it became around the time I finished high school and went off to college. The neighborhood kids were always going off into the woods to explore or swim or build a tree fort or just goof around. In the summer we caught fireflies in jars with holes poked through the lids so that they would be able to breathe, and Greg and I always managed to catch a frog or a toad so we could sneak up behind Penny with it and make her scream. We had a houseful of pets: a series of dogs, two or three cats at a time, a parakeet, a rabbit, a couple of guinea pigs, and several turtles who always seemed to end up wandering under kitchen appliances, never to be seen again. My sister kept bringing caterpillars home in shoe boxes hoping that, if she supplied the right combination of twigs, blades of grass, and dandelion puffs, one of them would spin a cocoon and turn into a butterfly. I brought her a branch with a cocoon hanging off it once and we put it into one of the firefly jars, but whatever was growing inside it never came out.

Since I was the oldest, I went off to the University of Pennsylvania expecting to carry on the traditional family profession. I had never been particularly interested in medicine, but I had never really thought much about following a different path, either. It was just a foregone conclusion that I went along with until I was away from home and realized how much I didn't want to go along with it. President Kennedy had just established the Peace Corps, and one of my classmates decided to postpone his sophomore year so that he could go to Africa to teach groups of villagers how to set up rudimentary irrigation systems. The idea of making that kind of a difference in people's lives really appealed to me. But it was clear from my father's silence during Thanksgiving dinner as I went on and on about the Peace Corps that he was not in favor of my acting on this impulse.

I went back to college and started spending less time studying and more time carousing. I guess this was the first time that I used liquor to disguise how discontented and trapped I was feeling. But before I had a chance to flunk out, I met and fell in love with a Fine Arts major named Marcy. She was a cellist and she always wore black, with her dark hair scraped back from her face into a ponytail so that it would not be in her way when she leaned forward over her instrument to play. The austerity of this look, and the fact that she only wore eye makeup, made her green eyes even more striking. She introduced me to chamber music and Shakespearean theater, and we enrolled in a Drama class together the following semester. After watching me act out a few scenes in class, Marcy encouraged me to audition for a Drama Club production of *The Importance of Being Earnest*. I actually got the first role I ever auditioned for, which was the minor part of the minister, Dr. Canon Chasuble.

Once I caught the acting bug, I made sure I participated in as many of the theatrical productions staged on campus as possible. I also got involved with a community theater group during summer break; it was the first time I chose not to go home for vacation. Surprisingly, my father was more supportive of this change of direction than he had been of my wanting to join the Peace Corps. My parents came to see me in my first starring role as the Gentleman Caller in a production of *The Glass Menagerie*, which was staged by the Drama Department at the end of my junior year. After the play, my father encouraged me to go to New York City for professional training.

"Don't expect it to be an easy way to make a living," he warned me. "But I think it makes more sense for you to try your hand at something that suits you than to keep trying to force yourself into someone else's pigeon hole."

It was the best advice I ever got.

D2

Since no other family member had ever attended college, her parents had not saved for Denise's education. The monetary gifts she received when she graduated from high school paid for her first semester at Charter Oak State University. After three semesters of working part-time in the shoe department at Marshall's in order to pay her full-time college tuition, she decided it was time to reverse her approach. She got a full-time office job at the Yale School of Forestry and enrolled in two courses that met in the evening at her own school.
    In keeping with the "rebel at all costs" philosophy she maintained throughout high school, Denise had opted out of the college prep program halfway through her junior year and enrolled in business courses. Many of her brainiest friends shared her convictions and admired her gutsiness, but continued along a more conventional path. Their parochial school was so strongly oriented toward college prep that time was set aside during regular school hours for all juniors and seniors to take PSATs, SATs, and ACTs, regardless of their future plans. When she shared her scores with her friends, they began a campaign to make her see reason.
    "You can't let scores like that go to waste!" "Do you have any idea how lucky you are?" "There must be some school somewhere that would at least be worth applying to." "Don't blow this chance—you can always change your mind later!" Her tough-minded sophomore English teacher, Sister Dolorita, came to her with tears in her eyes and

reminded her of the unprecedented perfect score she had achieved that year on the standardized English proficiency exam administered statewide. When she had called Denise up to her desk to see those test results, Sister had swept an upturned palm down the column of numbers and wryly remarked, "What more can I say?"

After weeks of unrelenting pressure, she reluctantly agreed to apply to just two schools. The state university system was the only realistic financial possibility. But the University of California at Berkeley appealed to both her radical views and her sense that the West Coast might be the right place for a diehard nonconformist like herself. She was accepted for admission by both schools, but reality had trumped nonconformity.

Her job at the School of Forestry entailed the same duties as any other secretarial job in any other workplace: seeing to the clerical needs of important men with big ideas whose lofty perch left them ill-equipped to divine the intricate workings of electric typewriters and Xerox copy machines. But the job put her amidst socially conscious, politically enlightened young people who literally danced and partied in the hallways the day Richard Nixon was driven out of office, and she was glad to be surrounded by like-minded people.

She was assigned to four professors, one of whom was away on sabbatical until after semester break in January. Professor Wheeler had a reputation for frightening the help, but Denise quickly discovered that all she needed to do to keep him from barking at her was to make him as inaccessible to other people as possible. She never put any of his telephone calls through to him, collecting a pile of pink While-You-Were-Out messages to be slipped under his office door at the end of each day. In the unlikely event that a student who had not been ordered to appear wanted to see him, she politely recited the tersely-worded response he had scrawled on the back of a Rolodex card and thrust at her on her first day: "He is out. He will not be returning today. Make an appointment to discuss the issue with your faculty advisor."

Professor Styron was quite the opposite, never happier than when he was listening to the sound of his own voice making sagacious pronouncements to some duly impressed student—unless he was enjoying the even greater treat of addressing a group of students. He was supremely narcissistic and self-important, chastising her for being unavailable the day after her beloved grandfather's funeral to make last-minute changes to an article he hoped to submit for publication later that month. "After all," he observed, "life is for the living."

Professor Jennings, who would become a Professor Emeritus at the end of the academic year, was a delightful gentleman who added very little to her workload because his days of writing articles, attending committee meetings, or even preparing for classes were behind him. Except for occasionally needing her to type up an arbitration agreement he had negotiated between a labor union and an environmentally irresponsible employer, he was most notable for his absence.

Their Christmas gifts reinforced her impressions of these men. Professor Wheeler gave her nothing; Professor Styron autographed the issue of the journal that contained his article; and Professor Jennings took her around the corner to the local Irish bar, Malone's, for lunch and a few belts.

P3

I spent two years in New York City studying comedy technique and the Method at the American Professional Theater Annex, or APTA. I also took classes in projection and elocution, movement, and fencing. After I had been at the school for about six months, I felt confident enough to start auditioning for small roles with small companies around the city.
     My first few jobs were with an amateur Shakespearean repertory company housed in a converted warehouse near Battery Park. After several walk-ons and bit parts, I got to play my first full-fledged character: Quince, the carpenter in *A Midsummer Night's Dream*. I spent the summer at the Eugene O'Neill Theater in Connecticut, both stage managing and understudying. The following fall, I finally got into Actors Equity when I landed a couple of minor roles in an off-Broadway production of three one-act plays by Chekhov, *The Bear*, *The Boor*, and *The Brute*. Back when Marcy and I were enrolled in that first Drama class, I had read about the colony of bohemians and artists who lived in Greenwich Village and founded the original Players Theater around the time of World War I. Having the opportunity to appear on that stage, and to do so as a member of Actors Equity, was a very gratifying experience.
     Marcy and I tried to keep our relationship going when I first got to New York, but the changes in our lives and the distance between us made it impossible to continue. I didn't have much to offer as a boyfriend at that point in my life anyway, because I was so focused

on my studies. When I wasn't in class, I was reading anything I could get my hands on about the craft of acting, or going to the theater to watch how the professionals did it, or meeting with other students to discuss technique. There was very little time in my life for socializing, but when I did spend time with girls they were people I knew from APTA who were as obsessed as I was with the theater. No one was interested in a long-term commitment; we all used each other for the moment and then moved on.

Once I was in Equity, a wider variety of job opportunities opened up for me. My first television appearance was as a guy with a splitting headache in a commercial for Bayer aspirin. I didn't have any lines, but I had to do a lot of grimacing in pain, and at the end I got to kiss the girl who was playing my wife. I also had a few bit parts in some of the old-style drama anthology programs that were still being aired at the time; when I was credited at all, it was usually as something like "Third Soldier," or "Tall Frat Boy." I even appeared in one of the educational films that used to be shown in elementary schools on those clunky old reel-to-reel projectors. I was Miles Standish in a dramatization of the legend of John Alden and Priscilla Mullins. I didn't get the girl, but at least I got the most lines.

My biggest break came a few months after I finished my studies at APTA, when I landed a role in a road company production of *Bus Stop*, by William Inge. The play had done well on Broadway in the mid-fifties, and was an even bigger hit when it was turned into a movie starring Marilyn Monroe. Probably because of the mystery that still surrounded her death almost three years later, we were booked for three- or four-day engagements all over the country, finishing up in Philadelphia about six months later. I played Dr. Lyman, a lecherous drunk who did not make it into the film version. I enjoyed creating a character who was not the usual one-dimensional "type" that supporting characters often become. I played him as someone who has lost his position in society, but not his innate dignity. His charm somehow makes up for his dissipation, but at the same time he uses that charm to take advantage of the innocent waitress he is after. I had a good time flirting with the actress who played that waitress, Wendy Raymond, both on and offstage. I also got a kick out of portraying a doctor, since I had so many of my father's dinnertime anecdotes to draw upon. Best of all, it was great to have so much time with the rest of the cast—a group of people with whom I shared so many common interests and concerns, and who were always there to applaud each other's efforts or, if necessary, to lend moral support over a drink or two.

Since the tour ended in Philadelphia, I decided to go home for a long overdue visit. I missed my family, and I wanted to be in the best place I could think of in order to decide what to do next. I had to choose which path I wanted my career to follow: theater, or film; New York, or Hollywood. I spent a lot of time revisiting the woods and the mountains where so many of my childhood memories were created. The tranquility of home and the solitude of the landscape freed me from the day-to-day worries that would have been such a distraction if I had gone straight back to my apartment in the city. In the end, I realized how important the natural environment was to me, and I knew that I would be miserable if all I could see out my window was skyscrapers. So I chose to go west.

D3

Because he was the youngest member of the faculty, Professor Harry Thorpe was one of the most popular instructors at the School of Forestry. He wore his sandy brown hair long and shaggy, and came to work in blue jeans most of the time unless he had a particularly important meeting to attend. On those days, he would wear corduroy jeans and a sport coat. He was not quite handsome, but he had a style and an energy about him that attracted attention. He was also married and the father of a four-year-old son.

Professor Thorpe had returned from his sabbatical in Germany's Black Forest region with a major project for his new secretary. On his first day back, he deposited a battered Xerox paper carton in the middle of his office floor. Beneath its lid lay the handwritten manuscript of his contribution to a new textbook being assembled by an associate at the University of Southern California. The purpose of the book was to approach the traditional areas of instruction in forest management from a more ecologically-enlightened point of view. All of the manuscripts were to be submitted by the last week of February, so that a publication date for the book could be announced on Earth Day.

Once she got familiar with Professor Thorpe's handwriting, Denise was able to finish typing up an entire yellow legal pad full of notes by lunchtime each day. He would review what she had typed and make whatever revisions he thought were called for while she completed whatever work needed to be done for the other professors. Then she would go to work on Professor Thorpe's revisions, and file the new pages with the rest of the final draft by the end of the day. In this way, they were able to make a great deal of progress in a relatively short time.

Since they were spending so much time together, their conversations soon progressed from all-business to casually friendly. In those days, political views were a kind of shorthand for personal identity, and they quickly learned that they were in agreement on the major issues of the day: the war, the environment, and Watergate. Soon they had exchanged personal histories and family background information, and eventually began to confide in one another about what was going on in their private lives. Denise knew that there was something vaguely inappropriate about these conversations, but she was nevertheless flattered by the attention and grateful for the diversion.

One Friday afternoon, as she was walking down the corridor on her way to the mailroom, she heard a soft moan behind her. She did not turn around to see who was following her because she assumed it was a student making a clumsy move on her. The students at the School were almost exclusively male, and it was not unusual for them to periodically poke their heads up from behind their textbooks and notice the predominantly young secretarial staff. But then a student came around the corner, greeted the person behind her, and walked over for a brief conversation. Smiling to herself at the moaner's bad luck, she glanced back before she entered the mailroom and saw Professor Thorpe talking with the student.

Although she had become friendly with the other woman in her office, a fortyish divorcee named Anita, Denise was neither too young nor too inexperienced to realize that this was not the kind of information to be shared with a co-worker. But youth and inexperience also allowed her to be more amused than offended by the incident. She did not take the idea of her boss moaning at the sight of her very seriously; she saw it as a way of relieving some of the boredom of the workday. She concluded that she could wring the most entertainment out of the situation by feigning ignorance and waiting to see what might happen next.

The following Monday, Professor Thorpe deviated from their usual work routine. Around mid-morning, he buzzed the intercom and asked her to come into his office for some dictation. Once she was settled in a chair opposite his mahogany desk, he explained that since they were making such good progress on the manuscript, he thought it would be all right to take some time away from that project to catch up on some of his correspondence. After dictating three memos, he got up from behind the desk and walked around to lean against the front of it. After several letters, he asked her about her weekend. Denise told him about some of the more interesting people she had met at Malone's, which had become her regular Friday night hang-out, and he told her about a party he had attended at another professor's home. There were a few seconds of silence, and then he asked if she would mind if he kissed her.

"No, I wouldn't mind," she heard herself reply. He leaned down and ran the backs of his fingers along her jaw and under her chin, tilting her face up toward his. After a few moments of considerable neck strain, he took hold of her upper arms, raised her to her feet and pulled her against him.

P4

I had only been in Los Angeles for a few weeks when I signed on with an agent. A friend from APTA had spoken with his agent about me, and gave me the telephone number of the agency so that I could call and set up an appointment as soon as I arrived. From the first time I met Ben Holzer, I felt like he got who I was and what I wanted to do with my career. I don't know if it was because of what my friend had told him about me, or if it was just one of those instant connections that happen between people sometimes. He laid out a plan for me that involved slowly putting together a body of work consisting of bigger and bigger roles, with the objective of making my face recognizable enough to land a contract with one of the major studios.

There were still quite a few westerns being broadcast at this time, and my first West Coast television appearance was a bit part on the longest running of them all, "Gunsmoke." I played a nameless member of an outlaw gang with a couple of nondescript lines like, "I reckon so, Jeb," and "We ride out at sun-up." On "Bonanza," my character competed for the affections of the girl Little Joe was in love with that week, and took a classic cowboy punch to the jaw during a saloon brawl. I also appeared as soldiers on several World War II-era dramas, as well as lots of guys in trouble with the law.

While none of this work was rewarding on an artistic level, it provided enough income to pay for a secondhand Ford Mustang and the rent on a small studio apartment above a storefront in West

Hollywood. I started exploring the areas outside of the city when I was not working. At first, I spent a lot of time at the beach because I had never lived so close to the ocean before. I tried to get there either first thing in the morning or toward dusk, in order to avoid the crowds of surfers and beach bunnies who blocked the view and blasted their transistor radios all day. When the beach was empty, the sounds of the surf and the reflection of the sunlight on the waves were peaceful and relaxing. But the shore did not speak to me the way woodlands and mountains did, so I went looking for that kind of landscape. When I discovered the High Sierras, I felt like I was home again.

I met a lot of girls during those first few months, but once I got past the initial physical attraction I found that I did not have much in common with them. Almost all of them were either already in show business or trying like mad to get into show business, but they did not seem to have the same commitment to their work that I had. They looked at acting as a means to an end, rather than as a valuable experience in and of itself. So while I did not lack for feminine contact, I was pretty lonely.

Ben's plan came through in less than a year, and I found myself under contract with Film Gems, the television division of Apex Studios. This meant that I could now count on a weekly income, which allowed me to move into a slightly larger apartment a little farther outside of the city. It was a multi-family complex with a good sized yard and neighbors both upstairs and on either side, so I felt much less isolated than I had in West Hollywood. Other than one young married couple, everyone living there at the time was single so it was kind of like living in a college dormitory again. People were in and out of each other's apartments or hanging out in the yard together all the time, usually getting high. I ended up staying in this apartment for over five years, and I saw a lot of people come and go during that time. But that first group was exceptionally tight; in fact, quite a few stayed in touch long after they moved away.

I met Sandy at a birthday party my neighbor Tracy threw for her boyfriend. He and Sandy's brother, Tom, were musicians who had gotten friendly back when they were both washing dishes at the same restaurant. They started spending a lot of time jamming at Tom's place, and Tracy and Sandy had become good friends.

The first time I saw Sandy, it was like one of those scenes in a movie when the guy sees the girl across a crowded room and everything around them seems to come to a halt. She was one of the most beautiful girls I had ever seen, even with the long blonde hair and blue eyes that just about every girl in L.A. seemed to have at that time. She was wearing an extremely short miniskirt, and her legs were long and sexy. But there was something even more compelling about her than her appearance that I still have a hard time putting into words. I caught sight of Tracy and practically sprinted over to ask her to introduce us. She linked arms with me and we walked over to where Sandy was sitting on her own, a little apart from the crowd, bobbing her head and tapping her foot in time with "Itchycoo Park."

"Hey, Sandy," she said. "This is the downstairs neighbor I've been telling you about who is so good about putting up with Mark's noise."

Sandy stood up, held out her hand to me, and smiled—and I was hooked.

D4

Denise learned a lot from Harry. He was thirteen years older than she was, and he tried hard to steer her clear of some of the classic pitfalls of youth. He advised her not to let anything get in the way of completing her Bachelor's degree. He warned her about the self-absorption of young men her age, and urged her not to let anyone force her to settle for anything less than what she truly wanted in life. He even shared some of his favorite books with her, as well as his considerable knowledge of his field.

But she also learned from Harry that even young, hip married men resorted to the same old lines that married men always used on single women. "My wife doesn't understand me." "We hardly ever have sex." "I only stay because of the child/children/financial ramifications/suicide threats." The odd thing was that Denise never gave Harry any reason to believe that she needed to hear any of these standard-issue statements. But he seemed compelled to utter them, and the banality of these lies made something that was supposed to be fun seem tawdry.

She told him that she had experienced an attack of conscience, and that she did not feel right doing what she was doing to another woman. Since her father had repeatedly been unfaithful to her mother over the course of their twenty-five year marriage, her conscience had in fact been bothering her. The nagging feeling that she was somehow betraying her mother had been trying to elbow its way between Harry and her all along. But the decision to call a halt to the affair had more to do with how it made her feel about herself than it did with feeling guilty about her actions. Denise had begun to feel as though she were a character in a badly written, clichéd first novel that had been relegated to a bookstore remainders bin. Somewhere along the line, she had stopped feeling that she was not good enough and realized that she was better than this.

Her friendship with Anita had suffered as a result of her involvement with Harry; although the situation was never directly addressed, was clear that the woman knew what was going on and disapproved wholeheartedly. So when a position opened up in the Dean's Office, Denise applied for a transfer. On the strength of written recommendations from Professor Jennings and Harry, she got the promotion.

During the time that she was working at Yale, Denise used her employee tuition reimbursement benefit to finance the completion of her Bachelor's degree in English Literature. It took several years to accomplish this task because her full-time workload at the School of Forestry made it impossible to carry more than a course or two each semester. Once she had achieved her goal, she resigned from the University in order to search for more meaningful employment.

Her politics had mellowed somewhat with time, although she held true to the same core beliefs she had embraced in the past. But she had quickly worn her idealism out trying to convince the government via demonstrations, or voters via campaign canvassing, to see things her way. Instead, she focused her energy on making a worthwhile contribution to society by living a socially responsible life and encouraging the people around her to do the same. She refused to buy products manufactured by companies that tested on animals, participated in beach clean-ups, turned the thermostat down and the lights out, and reused or recycled nearly everything that could not be composted.

After casting about for a direction, Denise became the editor of the monthly newsletter for a non-profit advocacy agency for the disabled. She worked closely with the caseworker advocates on staff as well as administrators and members of the Board of Directors. Through her interactions with both clients and co-workers, she gained a great deal of insight into the many forms of discrimination and inaccessibility that disabled people encountered in their daily lives. After researching her options, she decided to apply her aptitude for language to learning American Sign Language so that she could be trained as a sign language interpreter.

P5

I started appearing regularly on a situation comedy entitled, "Tammy," which was based on the old movie starring Debbie Reynolds. Both the film and the TV show were about a backwoods country girl who comes to live with her sweetheart's snooty family in their antebellum mansion, and eventually wins them over with her simple, folksy ways. I played the leading man's brother, a character who was not featured in every episode. However, I did appear in twenty of the thirty-two shows that were filmed for the one season that the series aired. This got me into the public eye on a regular basis, and provided me with quite a bit of exposure to the powers-that-be at the studio. As a result, I was put on the fast track for the upcoming pilot season and did my first fan magazine interview.

Ben had prepped me for the interview, and sat just a few feet away throughout the thirty minutes or so it took for me to relate my life story to the reporter from *Screen Time* magazine. It was the strangest experience of my life up to that point. I understood the importance of publicity to a successful career in Hollywood, and I was willing to play the game in order to get to where I wanted to be. But having a conversation consisting of rehearsed answers to stock questions was not something I had been trained for at APTA. It wasn't until the very end, when the interviewer asked me what I most wanted my "fans" to know about me that I had a chance to speak freely. I said, "Acting is a difficult profession, but I enjoy it. If I can help people forget their troubles for a little while, then I feel like I've made a small, positive contribution to society. If everyone could love what they do for a living as much as I do, the world would be a much happier place." I guess my answer was a lot more serious than what the interviewer was looking for, because none of these comments made it into the article.

I had been especially uncomfortable with the amount of interest the interviewer had in my love life. This was just after Ben and I had one of the few major disagreements that I can remember during the time he represented me. He had wanted me to participate in a photo shoot with an actress who would be posing as my girlfriend. There would be a series of semi-intimate shots of the two of us which Ben would then shop around to the fan magazines; ideally, one of them would publish a two-page spread. I flat out refused to go along with the idea. Sandy and I had just started dating, but I would not have agreed to it even if that were not the case. It was just too phony for me.

I did agree to escort actresses who were also under contract with Apex to various industry events. Photographs from movie premieres, award shows, and parties were always turning up in trade and local newspapers, and that kind of exposure was vital to someone in my position. It was important for my face to be known, and to always appear to be as photogenic as possible. I was able to reconcile myself to participating in this kind of charade because I did not feel that I was being deliberately deceptive. I had no control over whether or not people who saw the photos assumed that there was something going on between the actress and me just because we had attended an event together.

Sandy was amazing about all this. She accepted that it was an unfortunate part of the business I was in, and it never seemed to make her feel jealous or threatened in any way. The maturity with which she handled my being required to "date" other women was particularly impressive considering how young she was. I think a lot of other women would have objected, and it would have been perfectly understandable for someone to react that way. But Sandy was not like any other woman I had ever known in so many ways.

Her father had been critically injured in a car crash involving a drunk driver a few years before we met, and her mother's life had been dedicated to his round-the-clock care ever since. Sandy had come to stay with her brother in L.A. after high school, with the intention of enrolling at UCLA. Instead, she was pursuing a career in dance, which she had studied for years back home on Long Island. When we met, there was no way I could have guessed that she was a few months shy of her twenty-first birthday. There was a steadiness and a serenity to her far beyond what someone her age would ordinarily be expected to possess. Considering her family history, the effortless grace with which she lived her life was even more remarkable.

To be honest, I was a little uneasy when I first found out about Sandy's age. Since our birthdays were nine months apart, I was nearly five years older; but more importantly, she was still a minor. Ben was worried about what would happen if that fact became public knowledge. He told me that any kind of negative publicity could be fatal at this stage of my career, when I had neither an established reputation within the business nor a loyal fan base eager to see my work.

But after we had been together for a few months, I felt like Sandy was the one person outside of my family with whom I was most able to be myself. And the more I felt like I was being folded, spindled, and mutilated by the Hollywood machine, the more important it became to me to stay in touch with my true self. So as time went on, being with Sandy meant more and more to me.

D5

The closest interpreter training program was located an hour and fifteen minutes away from where Denise was living in New Haven. She had to attend classes from 3:00 to 7:30 p.m. three times a week and, since she was driving into the northwest hills of Connecticut, she was often driving in a snowstorm along poorly lit, barely traveled roads. Furthermore, the training was more challenging than she had expected. Learning the expressive component of the language was not a problem, but understanding native signers did not come easily to her. This particular skill required a certain amount of natural ability for which intensive study was a poor substitute; for the first time in her life, she worried that she might not be able to attain a goal she had set for herself.

She was living in a rented condominium with her boyfriend, Dave, a quintessential nice guy with a good job in management at Sikorsky Aircraft. On the surface, they did not appear to have much in common beyond their genuine affection for each other. Their values and expectations for the future covered little common ground. But they enjoyed going to rock concerts and baseball games together, and shared a quiet intensity of purpose. For the time being, it was enough.

She got her first job as a professional interpreter several months before she completed the two-year training program. An elementary school on the southeastern shoreline needed someone to work with a deaf second grader. The first three months of the school year had already passed, and the school system was desperate to hire someone before the town could be found in violation of the federal Individuals with Disabilities Education Act. This law mandated that handicapped children be educated in the "least restrictive environment," meaning that they must be educated alongside non-handicapped children unless the severity of their disability would impede the learning process in a regular classroom. In this case, the law required that an interpreter be present at all times to facilitate communication between the student and his teacher and classmates.

Denise was interviewed by the head of the Pupil Services Office, who then led her down a long, cinderblock corridor to a large, noisy classroom. Twenty or so three foot tall children were arranged in groups of four around worktables. Windows stretched across the far wall from the tops of the radiators to the ceiling, and a door at the end of the wall opened out onto a broad, open field.

The deaf student, Enzo, was heavyset and sat apart from most of the other children. He wore thick eyeglasses in addition to his FM unit, a small, rectangular receiver that hung around his neck with wires running to each ear. The unit worked like a closed-circuit radio, eliminating all sound other than the teacher's voice as she spoke into a small microphone clipped to her lapel. Enzo took an immediate liking to Denise, most likely because she was the only person in the room that he could understand. He slipped his sweaty, pudgy little hand into hers when it was time to line up for recess, and she knew at once that this was a place where she could make a difference.

Her new career officially began on the morning after John Lennon was murdered. It was a strange day, with so many people her age stumbling toward each other in a daze, grasping at ways to reconnect with the consolation of the past. But she spent the day in a completely new environment, with people she had never met, doing a job she had never done before. For Denise, the day marked a beginning as well as an ending.

P6

After "Tammy" ended, I took a few weeks off and brought Sandy home to Patterson with me for a visit. My family enthusiastically welcomed her. Even our old dog, Rafferty, took to parking himself beside her and resting his head on her foot whenever she sat down in one place for more than a few minutes.

"What a lovely girl," my mother remarked as she watched Sandy teaching my cousin Kate's six-year-old daughter a modified pirouette.

I followed my mother's gaze, and then beamed at her in agreement.

"So kind-hearted, and so natural," she continued. Then she turned to me and said, "She's very—oh, what's the word I'm looking for?" She closed her eyes for a second and found it. "She's genuine!"

"I'm really glad you like her, Mom," I said. Giggles drifted over from the two dancers toward us. I turned back to them, smiled to myself and said, "She's the best thing that's ever happened to me."

By the time we headed back for pilot season, everyone had fallen under Sandy's spell and I was more in love with her than ever. I asked her to move in with me on the one-year anniversary of the day we met at Tracy's party. It was a tight fit with just two rooms besides the kitchenette and the bathroom, but we made it work. We turned the large combination living and dining room into our bedroom, and cordoned off opposite corners to create a private space for each of us. I attached a bank of mirrors to the wall behind a screen where Sandy could do her morning stretches and rehearse her dance combinations. My corner consisted of two bookcases at right angles to the walls with a pile of oversized pillows on the floor, where I could go over scripts or whatever political manifesto I happened to be reading at the time.

I went from a featured role in a failed sitcom to a starring role in a new one, entitled "Without Reservation." The series was to be filmed in Los Angeles but was set in Palm Springs, so we would periodically be going out to the desert to shoot some exterior scenes. I played a young newlywed who finds himself running the family hotel business despite having sworn to make his own way in the world. The show was actually pretty well written for its time, touching upon issues like independence versus family loyalty, and the struggles young married couples go through when they are trying to balance the two. Of course, each crisis was played for laughs and neatly resolved by the end of the episode, but I thought the show made some valuable points nonetheless.

My wife was portrayed by a cute actress named Mimi Yarborough, and we spent a lot of time kissing and hugging for the cameras. On our second location shoot, after we had been filming the series for couple of months, we spent the day in our bathing suits frolicking in and around a hotel swimming pool. We decided to have dinner together that night to run lines for the next episode, but ended up having a few too many cocktails to be able to really concentrate on the script. I helped her to her room because she was having a little trouble walking a straight line, and I ended up staying the night.

I felt so ashamed that I could barely stand to look at myself the next morning. I told Mimi that I thought Sandy had a right to know what I had done, but she said easing my conscience that way would only cause the woman I loved unnecessary pain. She made me believe that nothing would have happened if we had not been drinking, and since I was scared to death of how Sandy would react, Mimi did not have a very hard time persuading me to keep my mouth shut. Knowing how much the truth would hurt Sandy was enough to convince me that I was right to keep this one mistake to myself.

But it was not enough to keep me from making the same mistake again on our next location shoot. I had made sure that I did not allow myself to confuse fantasy with reality during our scenes this time. I also made a point of making dinner plans with a couple of the guys from the crew. But I drank even more while I was out with them, and when I headed up to my room for the night I found myself at Mimi's door again. To make matters worse, Mimi interpreted this as proof that I was more interested in her than I was willing to admit. This time, instead of cautioning me to keep quiet, she urged me to think about what it was that I really wanted and to go after it.

I was at a loss to explain my actions to myself, much less to my girlfriend. There was no doubt in my mind that I loved Sandy more deeply and truly than I had ever loved anyone before. I would not have thought twice about wiping the floor with anyone who tried to hurt her in any way. But now I had done something unforgivably hurtful myself, and I didn't know how I could possibly make it right. In the end, I decided that the only decent course of action was to tell her the truth.

The look on her face haunted me for years. I had taken hold of her hand when I began my confession, and as she realized what I was saying she carefully removed her hand from my grasp. Her expression changed almost imperceptibly from incomprehension to despair, and tears spilled over the edges of her eyes. I felt my throat close up and my eyes begin to sting, but before I could say another word she stood up, grasped the edge of the table to steady herself, and then turned and walked out of my life.

D6

After six years of smooth, rudderless sailing, Denise and Dave decided to call it quits. Over the course of those years, they had never made any specific plans for the future. It seemed that whenever he was ready to settle down she was not, and whenever she was ready to formalize their relationship he was noncommittal. Ultimately, their fondness for each other and the comfortable familiarity of each other's company could not override the fundamental differences between them.

One of those differences had to do with having children. Denise thoroughly enjoyed her daily interactions with the deaf and hearing students with whom she spent her workdays. In addition, she delighted in her new role as a devoted aunt to the three nephews who had been born over the past several years. These experiences had awakened her maternal instinct, making her long for a child of her own. At nearly thirty years old, the self-centeredness of youth had finally begun to recede, and she was ready to put a child's needs before her own.

Dave did not believe he had reached the point in his career that would allow him to financially support a family. He also did not see the need to rush into parenthood, since his own mother had given birth to her first child at thirty-five. More importantly, his parents had been messily divorced when he was only seven years old after his father had abandoned the family for a younger woman. This last, more crucial rationale was never verbalized, but they had been together long enough for Denise to know that it was at the root of Dave's reluctance. It remained unspoken because Dave used humor to ward off anything unpleasant. In fact, Denise could not remember their ever having discussed anything serious in depth at any time during their years together. They went their separate ways with a great deal of civility and very little regret.

After briefly considering visiting a sperm bank or adopting as a single parent, Denise decided to get a puppy. The result of an encounter between her brother's amiable male dog and a neighbor's good-looking female, the puppy was a mix of German Shepard, Alaskan sled dog, and Golden Retriever. Chloe grew to become the rare sort of dog that possessed all of the most desirable canine characteristics: beauty, brains, and benevolence.

Denise's self-image slowly folded itself into what she did for a living and her strong emotional bond with her nephews, the way blueberries get folded into a muffin mix. Like the hint of blue pervading the golden batter, her essence leached into everything that mattered most to her. But the more clearly defined aspects of her nature remained suspended within the limits of the life that she had marked out for herself. Chloe was the only living creature with whom she could break free of those limits, when they were running along the shore splashing through the ebb tide, or "dancing" together to Bonnie Raitt's bluesy laments on an otherwise solitary Saturday night. Over time, insecurity and disconnectedness crept out from the dark corners where they had stayed hidden for so many years and lurked in the shadows of her consciousness, waiting for an opportunity to pounce. She began to rely on a glass or two of wine every night to keep them at bay.

Eventually, she found that she could not drink enough to turn down the noise in her head and plunged headlong into her first major depression. On some days Denise found herself lying on the sofa unable to move for hours at a time, and Chloe would curl her body against hers, radiating warmth and solidity. When she was able to raise herself to an upright position, Chloe would run off to find her squeaky toy and gently nudge her into game of fetch. As the weeks dragged on, it became harder for Denise to recognize herself in the frightened, diminished image that peered back at her from the mirror.

It was the furrow of concern on her dog's brow that finally convinced her to make an appointment to see a doctor. Before he would write the prescription for an anti-depressant, the doctor made her promise not to use the pills to destroy herself. It was a promise she could readily swear to, but not because she felt morally opposed to suicide or obligated to the people in her life. She made the promise because she could never have turned her back on Chloe.

P7

"Without Reservation" was pulled from the schedule after just one season. The ratings were good, but the network opted to renew a series starring a former film star instead of our higher quality but lower star power show. Although it happened several months after the breakup with Sandy, I was still so shell-shocked that I barely noticed the cancellation.

Shell-shocked and drunk most of the time, as a matter of fact. This was the time of my life when I first discovered the effectiveness of alcohol as a memory aid—as in obliterating it. I was so filled with self-loathing that I set a chair in front of Sandy's mirrors so that I would be forced to watch as I drank myself into a stupor night after night. No one knew what had happened except for Ben, because I felt like I had to tell someone or I would explode. He was not a particularly insightful guy, but he really zeroed in on the truth of the matter when he asked me, "Why the hell would you do something so self-destructive?"

The question replayed over and over in my head, buzzing incessantly like a fly trapped between a window screen and the sash. I had an idea that if I could just figure out the answer, I would learn something important about myself that would help me to make peace with what I had done. But I was never able to come up with an explanation that sounded like anything more than a feeble excuse for something inexcusable.

I never showed up drunk on a set, and I was both lucky and unlucky enough to never suffer from hangovers. Lucky, because drinking never caused me to behave unprofessionally; unlucky, because I was able to hide it so well. The only time there was any hint that I had a problem was when I was stupid enough to get smashed and then get behind the wheel of a car. I was stopped twice for driving while under the influence, but I got off with a warning the first time and a $500.00 fine the second.

Ben started getting me guest appearances on various one-hour television dramas, which I really enjoyed doing. It was challenging and rewarding to me as an actor to create a wide variety of characters with different problems and motivations, much more so than portraying the same person week after week had been. It was also a relief not to be doing comedy at a time when I was feeling anything but light and carefree in my personal life. Some of the roles I played at this time turned out to be the best of my career and, as time went on, I found that I could focus on my work so completely that I did not need to drink nearly as much or as often as I had been.

By this time I had appeared in a few made-for-TV movies, some of which were nothing more than full-length unsold TV pilots. I finally broke into feature films when I won the role of a hip young priest who is tempted to leave the church when he falls in love with a free-spirited young woman. It was very difficult to make the move from television to movies at that time, because people in the industry had a tendency to categorize actors as right for either one or the other. I had been unaware of this practice when I had moved to L.A. from New York and made the switch from theater to television. I had expected to be able to progress easily from TV to film and, after a few years, to return to the theater. So to my mind, this opportunity was long overdue and I was determined to make the most of it.

The movie was called, "A Time to Every Season," and it was to be filmed on location in New York City. The fact that I would be able to get away from my usual surroundings for several months, and that I would be so close to home, was almost as exciting to me as actually landing the role. I flew east to visit with my family for a few days before I was due in New York. It was the weekend of the Woodstock music festival, and my father kidded me that I looked like I belonged there with the long hair and beard I had grown for the part of Father Tim. My mother worried that I was too pale, and my sister Penny took me aside and demanded to know why Sandy and I had broken up, and if that was the reason that I was looking so out of it. I could not bring myself to tell her what I had done, or how I had nearly drunk myself to death because of it.

"I'm okay now, Penny," I assured her. "This movie is going to be a whole new start for me." She looked at me dubiously, and rather than risk looking her in the eye I pulled her close and said, "It's almost a brand new decade, kiddo. Everything is going to work out fine."

D7

The first time it happened, she barely acknowledged it consciously. Although she was home alone, Denise thought she could feel someone approaching her from behind. There was no one there when she turned around, but one of her cats was staring intently at the place where she had just looked. Then the telephone rang and the moment was lost.

The same sensation came over her several times over the next few months. If she had not been off her anti-depressant medication for over a year, she might have telephoned her doctor to ask whether or not hallucinations were a common side effect. Instead, she put a call in to her Aunt Loretta, who was regarded as the family mystic.

According to family legend, Loretta had redecorated her kitchen with dozens of hanging baskets years ago and kept coming home to find the baskets strewn all over the floor. She and her husband checked and rechecked the hooks from which the baskets were hung, but she continued to find her kitchen in disarray whenever she returned to the house after an extended absence. A friend who claimed to have psychic abilities suggested that a restless spirit might be causing the mischief, and she suggested that Loretta start inviting the spirit to accompany her whenever she was going out.

Feeling silly, but willing to try anything in order to put an end to the chaos, Loretta said, "Come on, we're going out now," to the room the next time she had to leave the house for the afternoon. And to her amazement and relief, the kitchen was intact when she returned. It continued to remain so from then on, as long as she remembered to extend the invitation to join her whenever she left. Loretta had been interested in all things otherworldly ever since, and saw her friend on a regular basis for readings.

A few weeks later, Denise was sitting opposite the woman in a small enclosed porch at the back of her house. There was no table between them where mirrors, cheat sheets, or other sorts of aids might be hidden. The woman used no cards, tea leaves or any of the other familiar accoutrements of the trade, and did not accept money for her services. She said a simple prayer acknowledging that whatever might transpire was "by the grace and goodness of Jesus," and began talking.

Her first few remarks were somewhat general, but she soon came to more precise readings of signs pertaining to Denise alone. About halfway through the session, she told her that the spirit of an older man was around her. Denise nodded her head slightly, determined not to provide any inadvertent hints. The woman told her that the man had a cane, and that he wanted to reassure her that her financial concerns were unwarranted. She nodded again, her heart pounding with recognition.

Then the woman told her, "He says to tell you 5:00. He says, 'She'll know what it means.'"

Denise could barely retain her composure. Throughout her childhood and adolescence, her grandfather's unfailing support, acceptance, and love had made her strained, sometimes volatile relationship with her father easier to take. She had always felt more comfortable in his presence than with anyone else because she never felt that she had to do or say or be anything for Gramps. He sat back in his wooden rocking chair and enjoyed her just the way she was.

The signs the psychic read that day were all about him. Because he had served as the treasurer of his union local at United Aluminum and Smelting for years, he had always stressed the importance of keeping one's financial affairs in order. He used to tease Denise's grandmother that he planned to leave all his money to his granddaughter because he knew it would not "burn a hole in her pocket." As diabetes took first a toe, then a foot, and finally a leg, he had become dependent upon a cane. She had been grieving his loss since her days at Yale; he had died one cold February morning at approximately 5:00 a.m.

P8

The role of Father Tim opened a lot of doors that had been closed to me professionally. While the movie was not as popular as the filmmakers had hoped, it was seen by enough people in the industry to prove to them that I had the chops to move beyond television. Ben began carefully juggling television and movie scripts, so that I would be able to continue working without being pegged as just another TV actor again.

A perfect compromise came up when PBS began producing teleplays on the order of the old drama anthology series that were still around back when I was living in New York. Ben was able to get me a temporary release from Apex, and I was cast in the second play of the series as the Reverend John Hale, who comes to Salem to investigate the accusations of witchcraft in Arthur Miller's "The Crucible." Ordinarily, I would have been hesitant to portray another man of the cloth so soon after "A Time to Every Season." But the fact that they were being staged for PBS gave these plays considerably more prestige than if they had been aired on one of the commercial networks. In addition, a lot of well-known theater actors were cast in these plays instead of the usual stable of television personalities. I was pleased to discover that two of my old New York associates were involved in "The Crucible." Rich Stewart, who had been in several of my classes at APTA, was a member of the technical crew. And I had worked with Michelle Otis, the actress portraying Tituba the slave, at the Shakespeare repertory company in Battery Park.

The play was filmed in New York City, which brought me close to home once again. I stayed in the city on the weekends visiting with old friends, and I had a short fling with Michelle. I was still very raw emotionally from the breakup with Sandy, so it was good for me to finally be able to enjoy being with a woman again. The time I spent with Michelle helped me to heal, probably because it only went on for a clearly defined period of time, and with no strings attached. I still was not ready for anything more than that.

Once filming was complete I went down to Patterson for a few days. It was a much easier visit than the last one had been because my family could see how much healthier and happier I was. My father gave me a hard time about the fact that my hair was not much shorter than it had been when I was playing Father Tim, but that sort of conversation was probably taking place between thousands of fathers and sons all over the country at that time. My hair had not been short enough to satisfy my father since I stopped getting crew cuts back when I was a student at APTA.

I spent a lot of time during that visit exploring the places where I had spent so much of my time as a kid. I was surprised to see how few open fields were left, and how far the woods had been pushed back in just one year. It hurt to see the hills and the forest being bulldozed in the name of progress. That was when I decided to get involved with the ecology movement. I knew that there were a lot of groups in and around Los Angeles that were trying to make a difference at the grassroots level by sponsoring recycling campaigns and teach-ins. I made a commitment to myself to find a way to start contributing to the cause as soon as I got back.

It was not hard to find the information I needed. At that time, it seemed like concerned citizens were always handing out flyers to passersby or pinning up notices on community bulletin boards announcing meetings, sit-ins, and other types of gatherings in support or in protest of one issue or another. The day after my return from the East Coast, I went to the local library to look for reading material about the issues that most concerned me—conservation and air pollution. As I walked past the information kiosk that stood in the middle of the lobby, a giant circular poster painted blue and green to resemble the globe caught my eye. It announced that a meeting to organize local events for the upcoming national Earth Day was scheduled to take place in the library auditorium later that week.

I stayed up half that night reading the articles I had borrowed from the library, and went back the next day to look for more. By the time I got to the meeting that Thursday evening, I was pretty fired up about the mess mankind had made of the environment. I also felt proud and excited to be at the forefront of what I knew would have to be a continuing fight to clean up that mess. The members of our group were thrilled when several thousand people turned out on April 22 in support of our local observances. But when I watched the reports on the evening news that first Earth Day, it was mind-blowing to see how many millions of people felt the same way I did about such an important issue.

D8

When Denise's grandmother became too senile to live on her own, the family had no choice but to move her into a nursing home. For the first few months, her daughters had to explain why she could not go home every time their visits came to an end. After a time she forgot which home she had last left, and started asking if they had seen her mother. The three sisters gently, repeatedly broke the news to her that her mother was dead, and she mourned that death afresh every time, until Denise could stand it no longer.

"For God's sake, stop telling her that!" she demanded. "Just tell her Bella Nona is upstairs, or downstairs, or wherever her apartment was in relation to yours!"

Although she had been exceptionally close to her grandfather, Denise shared a special bond with her grandmother as well. The couple had moved into the house next door when Denise was three years old, and she spent so much time with them that the interior of their house was a more vivid memory than that of her own. It was amazing that two such dissimilar people had married and stayed together for nearly fifty years. Her grandmother would bustle around the kitchen, crackling with nervous energy, preparing Sunday dinner with her hat on because she was too distracted to remember to take it off after Mass. The calm eye at the center of the storm, her grandfather would sit reading the newspaper and smiling slightly to himself, occasionally raising his head and chuckling, "Take it easy, Ma."

In order to dispel her own fear of aging, Denise had chosen to believe it when people told her that memories were a great comfort to the elderly. But there was no way to reconcile this platitude with her grandmother's reality. Here was a woman for whom family had meant everything, and now she had no memory of any of the times she had shared with her children, grandchildren, or siblings. Soon she had no recollection of how they were related to her, although her eyes continued to light up with some reflexive recognition that went beyond thought whenever she saw them. Next she forgot who she was, and then how to speak. At that stage, the only mode of communication left was the sense of touch. Denise would hold her hand, or stroke her face, or kiss her cheek, and her grandmother would smile.

Denise refused to be knocked down by the relentless onslaught of losses that slowly, irrevocably wore her grandmother away. She would reel slightly and then right herself every time, steeling herself to assess what was left and adjust her expectations accordingly. It was not until a year after her grandmother's death that she found herself gasping for breath beneath another crushing depression.

Denise hated the idea of having to start taking medication again. She understood that her repeated bouts with depression had nothing to do with weakness of character or failure of will on her part. Her paternal grandmother had balanced on the edge of the same abyss throughout her life, and had bequeathed it to several of her children and grandchildren. Denise had simply come out on the losing end of a genetic crapshoot. But she deeply resented her powerlessness in the face of genetics, and once again tried to compensate for it with alcohol. She reasoned that if she used a bottle of wine to slow her descent into the dark, at least she would feel as though she had some control over her own life until the inevitable moment when she would have to give up and give in.

At the time, she was interpreting a U.S. History class at the local community college two mornings a week, and then driving to an elementary school in Fairfield County for a daily assignment with another overweight second grade boy. On a day when she had a little down time between jobs, she stopped by the cemetery where her grandparents were buried. The cemetery was located in a neighborhood that had deteriorated significantly since the time that the family plot had been purchased, so for safety reasons Denise did not get out of the car when she pulled up to their gravestone. She closed her eyes, said a quick prayer, and then spoke directly to them. "I miss you so much. I just wish you could let me know if you're really still there and can hear me."

On the long drive back from work that afternoon, she found herself obsessively thinking of death, decay, and hopelessness. They were the same images that had plagued her for weeks, whenever she was alone with her thoughts. A voice in her head sneered, "How pathetic and sad that people go to their graves believing that they possess an immortal soul. People are nothing more than highway road kill." Desperate for a little peace, she switched on the radio and was surprised to hear the long, slow opening of "Funeral for a Friend," by Elton John. The song was so lengthy that it was hardly ever played on the radio, but her brother had played it over and over on the 8-track tape deck in his car throughout the days of their grandfather's wake and funeral. When the song ended and the DJ began chattering, her black thoughts began to return so she stabbed at another button on the stereo.

The DJ on this station was saying, "We don't usually take requests during the week, but I just got a request for a song I haven't heard for a really long time. I like it when I get a chance to play a song I've forgotten all about. So here's 'All Things Must Pass' by George Harrison."

George had been Denise's favorite Beatle, and he generally did not get a lot of radio airplay. At first, she was distracted by the novelty of hearing one of his more obscure songs on the radio; she remembered reading somewhere that George had written it around the time of his mother's death, so it was not a particularly radio-friendly song. But after she listened to the lyrics of the first two verses, something began to dawn on her at last.

"Oh my God," she murmured, remembering her words at the cemetery earlier that day. At that moment, she was embraced by an intensely warm, comforting presence that seemed to rise up all around her, filling the interior of the car. She put a hand to her mouth as tears began to roll down her face. As the final chords of the song faded away, her black thoughts lifted and her sense of well-being was restored for the first time in weeks.

P9

I was still living in the same apartment I had been renting for almost five years, and my income had reached a level that was more than enough to cover my expenses. I decided to use some of my savings to buy an escape from the city sights and sounds that made me so uptight. I was looking for clear air, natural colors, and a little peace and quiet, and I found the perfect spot in the High Sierras. I bought several acres, and whenever I felt depressed or tempted to start drinking again, I headed for the mountains to get my head together. There was nothing better for me than lying in the shade of a tree while a breeze carrying the fragrance of pine and wildflowers rustled its leaves.

I found it very satisfying to be involved in trying to preserve the natural environment. As I became increasingly involved with different activist groups, I had the added pleasure of meeting a lot of people who shared my concerns and beliefs. I particularly enjoyed getting to know women who were passionately committed to something other than finding a husband or making it big in show business. Eventually, I started dating one of them.

Despite being born and raised in Los Angeles, neither Mary Ellen nor anyone in her family had ever had anything to do with the entertainment industry. It was very refreshing for me to be around someone who had her priorities straight. Our dates almost always involved doing something outdoors, often with her two dogs along for the ride. I had wanted to get a dog of my own for a long time, but my apartment was so small and I was away from home so much that it would not have been fair to the animal. Dating a devoted dog lover like Mary Ellen was the next best thing to having my own. Because she was a vegetarian, Mary Ellen got me to start eating health foods and taking vitamins. This had the added benefit of helping me to lose the few extra pounds I had put on when I was drinking, and got me feeling more positive and energetic than I had for a long time.

After another teleplay for PBS, I continued to do episodic television appearances in accordance with my contract with Apex. Whenever Ben arranged for me to be interviewed during this time, I made sure I found a way to work my concern for the environment into the conversation. Like many people of my generation, I believed that it was important to bring public attention to the important issues of the day; I was pleased that my career afforded me the means to do so on a broader scale than the average person. Eventually, I was approached by a representative of Green Peace who had been shown a copy of one of my interviews. The organization wanted me to narrate a documentary on whales that it hoped might be shown on public television. I was happy to donate my time to the project, and used my connections in New York to ultimately get the show aired by the local PBS affiliate. From there, it was picked up by WGBH in Boston, and was eventually broadcast nationally. Having an opportunity to use my reputation as a socially responsible actor in order to further the cause of conservation gave me a great sense of accomplishment.

The next feature film that I was offered was a spaghetti Western that was to be filmed in northern Italy. I would be playing the main character's colorful sidekick. Although it was not as big a role as Father Tim had been, the film seemed likely to be more effectively publicized and more widely distributed because it marked the directorial debut of a well-known Western character actor, Wes Donahue. The fact that I would be spending eight weeks in Italy was a very attractive added benefit.

Mary Ellen was not in favor of my taking the job. She did not see how I could justify going away for eight weeks when plans for the next Earth Day were at such a critical point. For the first time, her lack of knowledge of the entertainment business seemed like more of a disadvantage than an asset. The more I tried to explain the realities of what I did for a living, the more she dug her heels in. Finally, after several days of wrangling, she shouted at me, "I can't believe what a hypocrite you are! You talk a good game, but you're no better than all the other self-centered, conceited actors in this town!"

Before I had a chance to respond, she stormed off. I told myself that she did not mean what she had said, but I thought we could both use a cooling off period. I left for Italy ten days later fully expecting that, when I returned, I would be able to smooth things over.

D9

Working as an interpreter was unpredictable at best, but for once Denise knew for certain where she would be working for the next five years. Acting on a tip from her former supervisor at an interpreter referral service, she had been hired full-time by a suburban school system. She would be working with two eighth grade students as their interpreter/tutor, and would follow them to the high school. With long-term financial planning finally an option, she decided to buy her first home.

She looked at several available units in a condominium complex on the shoreline, less than fifteen minutes away from work. One of the reasons she had left the referral service was the fact that she had been continually assigned to schools in the middle of nowhere, often commuting for an hour first thing in the morning and again at the end of the day. When she was a young, eager interpreter, long commutes had not been a problem; as she became a more seasoned professional, she became less interested in extending herself to the breaking point. She felt that she had paid her dues and earned the luxury of a fifteen minute commute.

She was outbid on the unit she liked best, but the seller jumped at the offer Denise made for her second choice. The unit had just three rooms, but the view of the trees from the small balcony outside the kitchen was peaceful and private. Below the balcony, the full walkout basement opened onto a wide expanse of grass and, beyond that, wooded hiking trails alongside a narrow stream. This setup was perfect for Chloe. In addition, the full basement provided ample room for expansion if three rooms became too confining for the two cats, Chloe, and herself.

The job turned out to be one of her most enjoyable yet. The female student, Lisette, had used Cued Speech in school since kindergarten. She had requested a switch to sign language this year despite the fact that she used her own speaking voice to express herself both in school and at home. The parents of the boy, nicknamed K.C., had attempted to correct his hearing impairment with a cochlear implant two years earlier, but he refused to use it. At fourteen, Lisette was rebellious and difficult, but she came to view Denise as a trustworthy adult with whom she could let her guard down. K.C. was both exceptionally bright and intellectually curious; he was also a natural signer. Denise found working with them to be one of the most rewarding experiences of her career.

She had come to a comfortable place in her personal life as well. After twenty years of dating, Denise had had enough. "If I haven't been able to get it right after all this time, I never will," she shrugged. It was a relief to be able to call a halt to the search for a soulmate and focus on other, less demanding activities. She spent most of her free time bonding with her nephews, visiting with her friends, and communing with her animals, and would have happily continued to live her life in this manner indefinitely if Joel had not suddenly turned up.

Denise had been trying to find out where to have an Art Deco mirror that had belonged to her grandmother repaired. Lisette's homeroom teacher had met Joel when their daughters were in preschool together, before his ex-wife moved to Boston. Although his specialty was estate appraisal, Lisette's teacher thought he might be able to give Denise some guidance, or at least recommend someone who could.

Joel stopped by her condo on his way home from work one evening to take a look. After chatting casually for awhile, he asked whether or not she had eaten dinner yet.

"I still haven't gotten used to eating alone," he said. "Would you like to take a ride over to the diner with me?"

Denise had learned to avoid the awkwardness of eating alone by standing over the sink and gulping down her food as quickly as possible. Sitting down and chewing her food long enough to taste it sounded like a nice change of pace.

Six weeks later, Joel moved into the condo with her. They became engaged three months after they met, and four months after that they were married in a quick civil ceremony attended only by their parents and their two best friends. Joel stood apart from the other men Denise had known in lots of ways, but the most important difference was that he thought and behaved like a grown-up. When she gave up looking, Denise not only found someone for whom she was good enough, but who was also good enough for her.

P10

As it turned out, there would be no smoothing things out with Mary Ellen. If anything, she had become more convinced that we were not right for each other in my absence. I had probably never been as emotionally committed to her as I told myself I was, because I accepted her decision with very little argument. In consideration of her feelings as well as my own discomfort, I resigned from the environmental groups that we had joined together and got involved in George McGovern's fight for the presidency.

I spent the next six months traveling and campaigning intensively for the Democratic candidate. In Los Angeles, I did the typical grunt work of stuffing envelopes and canvassing neighborhoods. However, since I was reasonably well-known because of my many television appearances, the McGovern people also booked me for personal appearances in major cities all over the country. I was never the main draw at these events, but I did have a chance to make a brief statement whenever my turn at the podium came up.

While the war in Vietnam was the centerpiece of his political platform, my remarks always included my concerns for the environment and my belief that Senator McGovern shared and would address them if he became president. I told each audience, "Our complacency has gotten us into trouble, both in Vietnam and here at home. We've been self-indulgent and lazy, without any consideration of the damage we're doing to the planet. I believe it is our duty to try to clean up the mess we've made, and to realize that concern for the environment is not just a passing fad. There are two things we all need to do. First, vote for George McGovern." I would wait for the applause to die down here. "And second, find ways to get involved in making this country a cleaner, healthier place to live."

Unfortunately, all of our efforts were wasted and Richard Nixon was reelected in a landslide victory. This was a crushing disappointment and, coupled with the fact that I turned thirty that year, initiated a period of prolonged reflection on where I was at and where I was going with my life. I had met a girl named Suzanne when I was in Chicago for a McGovern rally, and there was an immediate, intense connection. Over the course of the campaign, we communicated daily and met for brief, passionate breaks whenever our schedules permitted. We got so carried away that we actually discussed marriage. Now, having put my career on hold for months only to be confronted with the cold reality of political defeat, I had some serious decisions to make.

As long as I was not physically near her, I could look at my relationship with Suzanne objectively. From a distance, I could see that it clearly bore too strong a resemblance to my involvement with Mary Ellen. I had never been interested in empty-headed Hollywood types, but I had learned the hard way that some knowledge and understanding of the entertainment business was necessary if a relationship with a woman was going to work for me. As much as I cared for Suzanne, our time together had existed apart from the every day circumstances and demands of my career. In the end, I chose not to run the risk of having what happened with Mary Ellen happen again, this time with a wife.

I returned to L.A. after spending Thanksgiving with my family in Patterson. Ben was not happy with the disappearing act I had pulled, but I convinced him that I was back for good and serious about getting my career on track again. I had to pay a fine for having been unavailable to work and therefore in violation of my contract with Apex, but Ben smoothed the worst of it over for me. I was soon back to work on a made-for-TV comedy-drama that was a pilot for a mid-season replacement series.

I was in New York filming a two-part episode of a detective show called "Streets of the City" when I got word that the pilot had been picked up and would replace a cancelled show on NBC beginning in late January. As far as I was concerned, this was not good news. I enjoyed the freedom of being a guest star, and had been hoping Apex would release me for a third PBS teleplay in the spring.

"You can't be serious," Ben said when I shared this idea. "After what you pulled with the McGovern thing, you were lucky I was able to get Apex to keep you on contract at all. You've got to spend at least a year keeping your nose clean and proving you can be a team player again before you start asking them for favors."

I knew he was right, but I dreaded the thought of being tied to one character indefinitely.

Ben put a reassuring hand on my shoulder as he walked me out of his office. "The odds are the show won't be picked up in the fall," he said. "Most of these mid-season replacements turn out to be just that. They almost never do well enough to be renewed for a full season. Just look at it as a short-term guaranteed payday."

The show was called "The Swindlers," and it was inspired by a Steve McQueen movie called "The Reivers" from a few years earlier. The film had been nominated for a couple of Academy Awards, and the script had been based on a William Faulkner novel, so the source material for the TV show was certainly a cut above what we had to work with on "Tammy." I had worked with members of both the production team and the technical crew during the years that I had been doing guest shots on various series. I had also really hit it off during the filming of the pilot with the actor who played my partner in crime, Dan McIntire, so the work environment seemed promising. I swallowed by pride, gritted my teeth, and crossed my fingers in the hope that Ben was right.

D10

Denise and Joel had only been married for a year when the subject of parenthood first came up, but they did not have the luxury of deferring the discussion because of their ages. With Joel's children living so far away, Denise thought that a baby might help to heal his heart. But as she neared her fortieth birthday, the prospect of pregnancy and childbirth was daunting. In the end, they decided to adopt.

They quickly discovered that their ages made them unlikely candidates for domestic adoption, and they found that they were ineligible to adopt from all but a few countries for reasons ranging from length of marriage to ethnic background. The final decision came down to a choice between China and Guatemala. Chinese babies were cared for in orphanages, while Guatemalan babies were placed in foster homes prior to adoption. China required a lengthy stay in country before adoptions could be finalized; Guatemalan babies could be escorted to Washington DC by an adoption agency representative. The choice was clear.

They began the process in January, when they hired a local agency called "A Child For Us" to do a homestudy consisting of a series of interviews, a home visit, and autobiographical essays. Once the homestudy was completed, they began the detailed, laborious task of assembling the necessary documents. This blizzard of paperwork included official copies of their fingerprints, birth and marriage certificates, property deeds, income statements, testimonials to their suitability as prospective parents, and medical reports attesting to their physical fitness. Each document had to be notarized, and then a document confirming the validity of the Notary's license had to be provided. After three months of chasing paper, entire sets were sent via FedEx to both the adoption agency in Maryland and the Guatemalan embassy in New York City.

They were notified in July that a baby girl had been born on June 12, and they were given ten days to decide whether or not they would accept this child for adoption. The only information the agency provided other than her birthdate was her weight and length. But Denise believed right away that this baby was meant to be theirs.

"She was born on the same date as my grandparents' wedding anniversary!" she exclaimed. "I know you don't believe in that kind of stuff, but it's got to be a sign."

"I never used to believe in that kind of stuff, but I have since I met you," Joel replied. "Remember how our song came on when we were picking out your engagement ring? What were the odds of that happening?"

Denise nodded, recalling the look on Joel's face when the jewelry store's piped-in pop schmaltz was interrupted by Debussy's "Claire de Lune" just as he slipped the diamond-encircled ruby ring on her finger. "So what do you think? Do we call and say we want her?"

Joel agreed, and a few days later they received the first photograph of their infant daughter. They got to work on turning a portion of the basement into a nursery for the baby as well as a new bedroom for themselves. Denise bought a book of baby names and began compiling a list of possible combinations. When they arrived at Dulles International Airport, the list had been narrowed down to just two. Denise said that they would know which one was the baby's name when they saw her.

As they hurried over to the terminal gate, they saw a dark-haired, brown-eyed baby in the escort's arms. Denise turned to Joel with tears in her eyes and asked, "Is that Belinda?"

Joel's eyes filled, too, and he squeezed Denise's hand and said, "That's her, all right."

P11

The series did surprisingly well opposite tough competition from the other networks, and at the end of the season NBC decided that "The Swindlers" would return in the fall. I had been completely cooperative and professional about the show, and had actually enjoyed doing it because everyone got along so well both on and off the set. But my ability to maintain a healthy perspective and live up to my end of the bargain had a lot to do with the faith I had put in Ben's prediction. Now, with the prospect of at least another 26 episodes looming over my foreseeable future, I was ready to pack up my things and disappear into the mountains forever.

"Take it easy," Ben pleaded as I stalked up and down the length of his office, fuming. "I told you that you would have to lay low and play the game for a year or so."

"It'll be a year in December, but I'll be stuck with this thing at least until next spring!" I shouted.

"I said a year *or so*. Nothing is ever carved in stone in this business."

"My gravestone will be," I snapped.

"Come on, don't talk like that," Ben said. Then he grumbled, "Jeez, you must be the only guy in town complaining to his agent that he has too much work."

"It's too much of the wrong work!"

"I know, I know." He crossed the room and came up to me, putting himself between me and the path I had been stomping into the carpet. "Look," he said reasonably. "Don't be crazy and walk away from this. You've got the whole summer to do whatever you want. I've got a couple of movie scripts here to show you—you can take your pick. If it runs over a little into the fall, I'll fix it with Apex. Don't even think about the series for the next couple of months."

I stuffed my hands down into my pockets and looked him in the eye. "How will you fix it?"

"Don't worry about that, I've got it covered. Just promise me you'll come back ready to give the series your best."

I shook my head in disgust, raked my hair back from my face with my fingers and said, "Right, right, right. So where are these scripts?"

I left two weeks later for the Philippines where I would be co-starring with Kenneth Davidson, a politically outspoken actor with enough clout to get a blatantly anti-war movie made despite the controversy it would create. I played a pot-smoking corporal who gets off on playing Russian roulette between firefights. He was the complete antithesis of my happy-go-lucky "Swindlers" character, and he put me in touch with some of the darkest and most deeply buried aspects of my own personality.

I returned to L.A. on time to begin shooting the new season of "The Swindlers." I had to be on the set by 7:00 a.m. every morning, and rarely left before 7:00 p.m. Since Dan and I were in virtually every scene of every episode, he and I worked almost nonstop all day, every twelve-hour day. For the first few weeks, I was too beat by the time I got home to do anything but choke down a sandwich and crawl into bed by 9:00. But I was usually too keyed up to sleep, so I started having a drink to help me relax.

I had been allowing myself to have a drink or two socially since Mary Ellen and I had broken up, but this was the first time I had drunk alone for years. I told myself it was no big deal as long as I kept it to just one drink, and that I was only doing it so that I could relax enough to fall asleep. I made sure I did not touch the stuff on the weekends by escaping into the mountains, where the natural surroundings soothed my restless mind and refreshed my spirit.

One Sunday evening on my way back to my apartment, I stopped at a produce market to pick up a few essentials for the coming week. As I was reaching across a bin choosing apples, I caught a glimpse of someone familiar on the other side of the aisle. When I looked up, there was Sandy lifting a bag of oranges into her shopping cart.

I was too nervous to speak to her at first, but when she started to push her cart farther down the aisle I took a deep breath and called out, "Sandy?"

She turned around, and I was touched to see a smile of genuine delight spread across her face when she recognized me. She said my name and wheeled her cart back toward the apple bins. "How are you?" she asked, in that lovely, warm voice that I remembered so well.

I nodded and lied, "I'm fine, thanks. How are you?"

She looked away for a fraction of a second, and then she shrugged and said, "You know how it is; some days are good and some are not so good."

I walked around the bins so that we would not have to talk across them. She looked at the groceries I had piled awkwardly in both arms and remarked, "Looks like you could use a cart."

"I think I'm coming in for two things and I always end up like this," I replied.

"Here, use mine," she said, "before you drop everything." She stepped aside to let me move closer to her cart.

I was afraid that her father's condition might account for her "not so good" days, so I asked how he was doing.

"The same," she sighed. We asked after each other's families and sent our best wishes to them, chatted about what Tracy was up to these days, and caught up on each other's careers as Sandy continued to shop. When we got to the check-out line, she told me, "I'm actually going to be relocating to San Francisco at the end of next month."

"Really?" I said. I kept my voice steady to cover how hard this hit me and asked, "What's in San Francisco?"

"A job with a very cutting edge modern dance company," she replied proudly.

I nodded, turning this information over in my mind as I lifted my groceries out of the cart and onto the conveyor belt. "I'm really happy for you, Sandy," I said, and I sounded so sincere that I almost convinced myself. After I paid the clerk and moved to the end of the counter, I said, "It sounds like you're finally getting the break you deserve."

"Well, it's been a long time coming, that's for sure," she said.

We walked out to the parking lot together, and I helped her load her bags into her Volkswagen Beetle. She thanked me and said, "It's been good to see you again."

I looked into her eyes and said, "It's been better for me." A look of concern flickered in her eyes for a moment, and she put her hand to my cheek. I put my hand over hers and brought the inside of her wrist to my lips. Then she looked up into my eyes and, very slowly and gently, I drew her into my arms and kissed her.

D11

"Mommy, the TV isn't working again!" Belinda called.

Denise slammed the knife she had been using down on the counter in frustration. "Good grief!" she muttered as she headed into the family room.

"See?" her daughter said, pointing at the solid blue screen's "Searching for satellite signal" message and the bar graph indicating that the search was not succeeding.

"I was just on the phone with these people for half an hour last night!" Denise exclaimed. For some reason, the satellite connection was working fine on the portable TV upstairs, but not on the main set in the family room. Denise had no idea how the same satellite dish pointed at the same patch of sky could produce two different results. She settled Belinda upstairs with a plate of peanut buttered banana wheels for a snack, and called DirecTV once again.

A serviceman was promised for the following afternoon. He inspected the dish on the roof, dried off a damp connection, and covered it with a waterproof seal. "This won't get wet again," he assured her as he flipped through the channels. Before his van reached the end of their cul de sac, the signal was out again. Denise sent Belinda tearing down the sidewalk to wave him back, and he reluctantly returned.

"Well, the only other option is to replace the receiver," he said. "But this work order does not authorize replacement equipment. You'll have to call Customer Service and schedule another service call."

"Can't I just call them now, since you're already here?" Denise implored.

He shook his head. "It's against Customer Service policy to deviate from our list of scheduled appointments."

Denise took a deep breath, counted to ten, and saw him to the door. She got another Customer Service representative on the line, who apologized profusely and scheduled a service call to replace the receiver for the following Monday. Denise pointed out that they had already been without service for more than a week and was redirected to a supervisor. After she related the saga yet again, the supervisor agreed to credit her account for the days they had been without service. Then the woman went even further and told Denise that she would authorize three free months of premium channel service as a way of compensating the family for their inconvenience.

That weekend, as Denise was looking over the channel guide to see if any movies she and Joel had missed might be airing on one of the premium channels, she noticed that the old TV show, "The Swindlers," was broadcast every afternoon on a specialty channel called "Bravo Gems."

"Oh, wow," she murmured, smiling to herself at the memory of the show and unconsciously slipping into an expression that had been a favorite of hers back when she had first watched it. Her delight at the thought of seeing the show again after so many years was tempered somewhat by the memory of its tragic history. But she went ahead and programmed her VCR to record the show weekdays at 4:00 p.m., and planned to watch the episodes later on in the evening after Joel and Belinda had gone to bed.

Denise was prepared to discover that the show had lost its charm over the years, and was pleasantly surprised to find that it had not. When she and her family left for a vacation in Toronto, she calculated that the series would reach episode 33—the point beyond which she had never been able to bring herself to watch—while they were away. She planned to simply delete those later episodes from the tape when she returned home. But when they got back, she found that none of the unwanted episodes had been recorded. There was still plenty of room left on the tape, and the VCR was still programmed to record daily at 4:00 p.m. She assumed that there must have been some happy technical accident and left it at that.

When the series restarted from the beginning a few weeks later, Denise decided that she had so enjoyed seeing it again that she would burn DVDs of the first half of its run. Their three-month period of free premium service was nearly over, but if she burned her own DVDs she would be able to share one of her old favorites with Belinda when she was a little older. She calculated the day on which episode 33 would air, but that evening when she tried to finalize the disk she discovered that the DVR plug had been pulled out of the wall outlet and was lying on the floor.

"Oh, no," she moaned. "How the hell did that happen?" She quickly ran through the possibilities in her mind. The door to the family room had been closed all day, so it could not have been one of the pets. Belinda had gone straight from school to a father/daughter soccer game with Joel. No one had been in the family room since she had watched "The Late Show with David Letterman" the night before.

Denise plugged in the DVR and turned it on disconsolately. When the finalization menu came up, she was shocked to see episode 33 appear on the disk contents screen. Once again, it seemed as if a combination of electronic malfunction and human miscalculation had conspired in her favor. But she was becoming less inclined to chalk all this up to coincidence.

Denise had been experiencing the vague sensation of a presence around her for several weeks, but she had less time to focus on that sort of thing now than when she was single. She had been profoundly grateful when tufts of Chloe's fur or her musky dog-scent would appear out of nowhere, at the precise moments when grief threatened to overcome her and the comfort of a wine glass beckoned. But the rest of the time she just told herself that her mind was playing tricks on her and went on multitasking.

Nevertheless, this sensation had not been easy to dismiss and an idea about its origin kept nagging in the back of her mind. Up until now, her theory had seemed too implausible to consider . . . but that plug could not have unplugged itself. She realized that the only person she could trust with such an unlikely story was her Aunt Loretta.

P12

Sandy and I spent a lot of time together during those six weeks before she moved to San Francisco. My twelve-hour days suddenly did not seem nearly so exhausting because I had her to look forward to almost every evening. We took things very slowly at first because there was a lot left unsaid between us that needed to be addressed. At the end of the first week, I decided to get everything out in the open.

We drove down to the beach on that warm, starry Friday night because I knew how much she loved being by the ocean. We clambered up onto a stone breaker and sat holding hands at the very top, with the wind sweeping the hair back from our faces. I fixed my gaze on the waves rolling up to the shore and told her about the tailspin I had gone into after we split up. Once I started talking, the words just poured out of me.

I told her how ashamed I was of taking the easy way out of my pain and guilt, drinking myself blind instead of facing what I had done to her, and to us. I told her how disgusted I was with myself for driving drunk after seeing what her father's accident had done to her family, and she leaned her forehead against my shoulder and squeezed my hand. Then I told her how hard I had to fight to get sober and to stay that way, and about how scared I was that I might be falling back into the abyss it had been so hard to escape. I felt myself beginning to fall apart, so I closed my eyes for a moment to compose myself. Sandy leaned over and kissed my cheek, and I turned to her and whispered, "I'm so sorry for betraying your trust in me."

"Sh-h-h," she said, touching her fingertips gently to my lips. "That's all behind us now," she said softly.

I searched her face for any trace of recrimination or disgust, but there was none. She reached over to smooth my hair back, and then moved close enough to press her lips behind my ear and run them down the side of my neck. We had been apart for such a long time that her touch nearly drove me crazy. I pulled her into my arms and let myself get lost in the warmth of her mouth and the taste of her skin. The more turned on I got, the more my shame and regret about the past seemed to just fall away.

We finally made love again that night, and spent most of the rest of the weekend in the same bed we had shared back when we were living together. We took all the time we needed to rediscover each other, falling back into old familiar ways and exploring new ones. I couldn't take my eyes off of her, or keep my hands to myself.

Sandy started getting worried about the way the grind of filming "The Swindlers" was affecting my state of mind. She encouraged me to look into finding a house to rent in one of the canyons on the outskirts of the city.

"You'd feel like you were out in the wilderness at the end of every day, instead of just on the weekends," she explained.

I agreed that a change of scene might help, and found a small two-story house on the edge of Topanga Canyon. The foundation of the building had been dug into the side of a hill, so that a ground level door at the front of the house actually opened into the forward part of the basement. To the left of the house, a steep flight of cement stairs led to the actual entrance in the back; to the right, two grassy hillocks sloped toward the street, ending at the edge of a wooded lot. It was quiet, private, and a perfect retreat from the grime and noise of the city. Sandy promised to leave some of her clothes there for when she could get away to spend a few days with me.

I desperately wanted her to change her mind about San Francisco, but there was no way I was going to ask her to stay when she had waited so long for a break like this. She had been involved with a well-known musician during the time we were apart, and he had always put his needs and his career before hers. I was determined not to make those kinds of demands on her, despite the fact that it hurt like hell to think of her being so far away.

On our last night together before she left, I tried hard not to let Sandy see how I really felt about it. I said all the things that I thought a supportive boyfriend ought to say, and tried to joke around a little. But eventually, I got very quiet. Sandy sat down on the sofa next to me and slipped her hand into mine, lacing our fingers together.

"I wish I didn't have to go," she said.

I kept my eyes focused on her hand entwined with mine and nodded grimly. "So do I." Then I turned to her. "But you have to do this."

"Maybe I don't—" she began.

"Yes, you do," I said firmly, squeezing her hand for emphasis. "You said yourself those two years with Stephen nearly buried you, professionally. This isn't just another job opportunity, it's a minor miracle. You can't walk away from it." I looked down again and shook my head in frustration. "If I weren't trapped here with this damned series, I'd move up there with you."

Sandy seemed to hesitate for a moment, and then she said "I know you could never really do that, but I love you for saying it."

Her voice was so soft I could barely hear it, and when I looked up I caught her brushing a tear from her cheek. "Yes I could do it, and I would!" I insisted. Then I took her face in my hands and said, "Don't you know I am so in love with you I can't see straight?"

After she left, I did my best not to become overwhelmed by the long hours and mediocre scripts I had to contend with on a daily basis. Renting the house really did make a difference; in the morning I could hear the birds singing instead of my neighbor's stereo blasting, and at night I could groove on the sounds of nature instead of cringing at the blare of traffic. But it was very isolated, and robberies were not uncommon because of the number of celebrities living in the more remote areas of the canyon. The Manson family murders were still a fresh memory as well, and I decided it might be a good idea to get a gun for protection. I wasn't sure if I could ever actually use it against an intruder, but just waving it around might be enough to scare someone away.

D12

Denise was sitting at the kitchen table with her favorite aunt. "The thing is," she began, "I've had experiences like this before with loved ones, but never with a stranger. I know you've read books about this kind of thing, and you've had a lot of experiences of your own. Have you ever heard of someone you don't know coming through?"

"Oh yes," Loretta replied. "Did I ever tell you what happened with my hairdresser?" Denise shook her head, and her aunt continued.

"I can see that poor girl now, standing behind me in the mirror telling me that her mother had died, and how guilty she was feeling because there had been a falling out of some kind between them. When I got home from the salon that day I started feeling someone around me, but I didn't make anything of it because someone is always passing through here—my husband, my daughter, even my pets. But then my cigarettes started disappearing. I'd turn the house upside down looking for a pack that I knew I had left on the dresser or the coffee table, and it would just be gone. I accused my family of doing it because they were trying to get me to quit, but they swore it wasn't them.

Then I started getting the urge to write. Now you know I've always loved to draw and paint, but I've never been a writer. And I'm right-handed, but I would sit down to make out a grocery list and I would find myself holding the pencil in my left hand! So I decided to just clear my mind of my own thoughts and let whatever was happening come out on the paper. It turned out to be a message from this girl's mother, and when I showed her what I had written she burst into tears because she said it looked like her mother's handwriting. I felt like I already knew the answer but I asked anyway and, sure enough, her mother was left-handed. And she hated being around smokers!"

"And this was someone you'd never met?" Denise asked.

"Never even heard her name before this happened."

"Well," Denise began. She then went into a detailed account of the events of the past several months, including incidents that she had not even acknowledged to herself before.

Her aunt seemed to anticipate some of what Denise had to say before she actually said it, and when she had finished, Loretta said, "Well, there is definitely something going on here. Did you know that spirits are drawn to energy sources like batteries and electronic equipment?"

Denise shook her head, and her aunt continued. "I've had a lot of that kind of thing happen here, with lights flashing and TVs turning on and off. There were a couple of occasions when I was visiting your cousin Charlie, and his caller ID showed a telephone call coming from this house when there was no one here. So that business with the VCR makes sense; they're attracted to all those kinds of things—computers, too. In fact, it probably goes back to when your satellite dish first started acting up—" Loretta broke off, and then said, "Someone is here right now."

Denise raised her eyebrows, and looked at the space between her aunt and herself.

"Yes, right there," Loretta said. "Do you feel that cold spot over there? I can feel it on my left arm."

"Yes, I do feel it," Denise replied, touching her hands to her cheeks. "The whole right side of my body is colder than the left side." She shivered a little and thought for a moment. "Sometimes it seems like this person wants me to know something, like I've been led to information I wasn't looking for, you know? But why would that be when I don't know anyone he might have a message for?"

Loretta sipped her tea thoughtfully, and Denise continued. "It's funny that you mentioned writing and computers, because I'm about to start an on-line creative writing course. Do you think maybe he wants me to write something for him?"

"Maybe," Loretta said.

Denise shook her head. "But why me? Why not someone in his family or someone he knew?"

"Maybe because you were open to letting him come through. Not everyone is like that, you know." Her aunt took her hand. "And time and space mean nothing on the other side, honey. Just because you didn't know him in this life doesn't mean there isn't some connection that you don't know about."

Before she had a chance to wrap her mind around this statement, Denise suddenly picked up the scent of pipe smoke. She sniffed again and asked her aunt, "Do you smell pipe smoke?"

Loretta sniffed the air and shook her head.

Denise sniffed a third time and said, "I smell pipe smoke."

Her aunt smiled. "Well, if you smell pipe smoke that's your Uncle Lou. He smoked cigars when we were out, but he smoked a pipe at home."

The two women were quiet for a moment, and then Denise asked, "So what do I do about all this?"

"Well, since you'll be writing for your class anyway, I think you should try speaking to him directly—be sure to use his name—and then just clear your mind and see what happens."

So on the first day of the semester, Denise stood in the middle of her family room and said, "Philip, if there is something that you want me to do for you, let me know what it is and I promise I will try my very best to do it."

P13

Sandy and I spoke over the telephone every night before we went to sleep. On the weekends, either she would spend Sunday with me in the mountains, or I would catch the redeye to San Francisco on Friday night and spend the weekend with her. Her birthday fell during Thanksgiving weekend that year, and she was able to get all four days off. We invited her brother Tom and his wife, our old friends Tracy and Mark, and Dan and his latest girlfriend to Thanksgiving dinner at the house. About halfway through, I looked over at Sandy and realized how happy I was just to be sitting across the table from her, entertaining friends together. I knew then that if I was ever going to get married, it would have to be to her.

December was a difficult month. The pace of filming the series was stepped up in order to make up for down time over the holidays, so we were actually shooting more than one episode at a time. There was absolutely no continuity, let alone time for rehearsal, and the scripts just seemed to get worse all the time. A year of my life was gone, and I was still stuck doing a job that I had come to detest. I started having trouble sleeping again, and I started having nightcaps to help me relax again.

Sandy did not have a lot of free time that month because her dance company was performing a modern version of "The Nutcracker" six days a week, right up until Christmas Eve. I had mixed emotions about us being apart so much of the time, because I felt lost without her but I didn't want her to know that I was drinking again. At least if we weren't together she didn't have to know what a screw-up I was.

The series finally broke for the holidays, and Sandy arrived on the morning of Christmas Eve for a ten-day stay. I tried to show some holiday spirit and act like everything was fine, but there was no fooling her. She took one look at me and knew I was lying.

"It's just been a rough couple of weeks," I said as I sank down on the arm of the sofa. "They practically worked us to death so they wouldn't fall behind schedule, and I feel like such a sell-out doing this show in the first place . . ." I put my hands on her hips and gave her a squeeze. "And I missed you so much."

Sandy sat on my lap and wrapped her arms around me, pulling my head down to rest on her shoulder. "I missed you, too," she murmured into my hair.

The next few days were great. We spent Christmas Day with Ben's family, and then we had all the time we wanted to do everything and nothing together. Since I didn't have to go to the set, I was almost able to forget about the series for the better part of a week. I made up my mind to start the new year off right by concentrating on sharing the things that made me happiest with the love of my life, and blocking out everything else. Then I made the mistake of watching the episode that aired that Wednesday night.

It was God awful, as far as I was concerned, and when it was over I totally flipped out. I was in such a rage that, when I finally stopped shouting and slamming and flinging things around the room, Sandy looked as though she was afraid of me.

"Oh God, baby, I'm so sorry," I said, and I crossed the room to where she was sitting. I held my hand out to her and she took it, but the look on her face really cut me up. "I'm just so wound up about this damned show! I'm sorry you had to see me like that."

She stood up and put her arms around me, nuzzling her head against my chest. Then she looked up at me and asked, "Why shouldn't I see you like that? If you're upset, or in pain, why shouldn't you be able to show it?"

I shook my head and said, "It's not right. I shouldn't be scaring you."

"I'm not afraid of you," she said. "I could never be afraid of you."

"I saw the look on your face," I said, and I pulled away.

Sandy grabbed my arm and yanked me back around to face her. "I wasn't afraid of you, Philip," she said adamantly. "I was afraid *for* you!" Then she threw her arms around my neck, and we held onto each other for a long time.

Finally, I felt myself relax a little in her arms and whispered, "It's late." I kissed the top of her head and ran my fingers down through her hair. Then I put a hand under her chin and tipped her face up toward mine. "Why don't you go up to bed?"

Something like alarm clouded her eyes and she asked, "Don't you want to come up with me?"

"I'll be in soon," I promised.

She hesitated, as if she wasn't sure whether or not to believe me, so I pulled her hard against me and gave her a deep, lingering kiss to convince her. It seemed to work, but she paused at the bottom of the stairs and turned to look back at me.

I smiled and said, "I love you," over the lump in my throat. Sandy smiled back, blew me a kiss, and climbed the stairs to our bedroom.

I waited until the sounds of her getting ready for bed had faded, and it had been quiet for fifteen minutes or so. Then I got out a bottle of whiskey and poured myself a glass. I knew I'd be having more than one that night, and eventually I set the glass down on the coffee table and just drank out of the bottle. The episode I had just seen played over and over in my head until the booze finally switched it off. Then I thought about my time in the Philippines, and I realized that the last time I had felt like a legitimate actor was when I was playing that crazy son of a bitch. I went into the bathroom to splash some water on my face, and in the mirror I saw the face of someone I despised: a fuck-up, a sell-out, and a drunk.

I don't remember making a conscious decision to take out the gun. I was so plastered by then that I do remember stumbling over my own feet when I was going up the stairs to get it. And I remember peeking in at Sandy asleep in our bed, with her blond hair spilling across her pillow and onto mine. Her hair was as pale as corn silk in the moonlight. For a moment, I thought about putting the gun away and curling up in bed beside her, slipping my arms around her and drinking in her scent.

But I didn't. I went downstairs and played Russian roulette instead.

D13

Several very long minutes passed with absolutely no response. No cold spot or enveloping warmth, no presence peering over her shoulder or messing with electronics.

Denise was deeply disappointed. She shook her head and muttered, "I guess maybe I really was imagining things." She waited a few more moments, unwilling to admit how much she had wanted to believe that the spirit of a stranger had actually chosen her from the great beyond for some special purpose. Then she started feeling embarrassed about having bought into such nonsense and thought, "Thank God the only person I talked to about this was my kooky aunt."

With a sigh, Denise shrugged and sat down at the computer. She logged onto the IClassroom website to check how much progress her writing buddy was making and sighed again, exasperated and disheartened. Mo was off and running already, no doubt turning out the nearly flawless prose that seemed to tumble out of her so effortlessly.

Denise logged off and opened a new Word document. She stared at the empty white screen without the slightest idea of where to begin. She sat motionless, until the screen went black and her reflection stared back at her for an instant, before the screensaver kicked in. She had no fall back plan. Without a story outline in her head or at least some notion of what she wanted to say, she knew that she would be spending a good portion of the semester in writers' hell—unless she just gave up and withdrew from the course, in which case she would spend months berating herself for being a quitter.

"Damn!" she grumbled to herself, closing her eyes and resting her face in her hands.

That's when she heard the first sentence. It was as clear as if it had been whispered in her ear. She shoved the mouse aside to switch off the screensaver, dropped her hands to the keyboard and began to type: "I can see now that getting drunk kept me functioning as well as I did for as long as I did."

Edwards Brothers Malloy
Thorofare, NJ USA
June 27, 2012